What Did They See?

ELVIS
GRUNDOON'S
ANTIQUES
+
CURIOSITIES

For Celia, Nina, Asher, Michael, Elise, Ilana, Vincent, Nasya, E'lon, Richard, Farrah, Ben, Ethan, Drew, Zena, Nathan, Eve, Lila, Emily, Jack, and special thanks to James K. M. Watts —J. S.

To Larry Brimner, a friend and fine writer, who reflects his good humor in our lives —D. C.

Henry Holt and Company, LLC / Publishers since 1866
175 Fifth Avenue / New York, New York 10010 / www.HenryHoltKids.com

Henry Holt® is a registered trademark of Henry Holt and Company, LLC.
Text copyright © 2003 by John Schindel
Illustrations copyright © 2003 by Doug Cushman
All rights reserved. Distributed in Canada by H. B. Fenn and Company Ltd.

Library of Congress Cataloging-in-Publication Data
Schindel, John. What did they see? / John Schindel; illustrated by Doug Cushman.
Summary: Raccoon hurries to show Beaver, Porcupine, and Otter the most
amazing thingamajig that they have ever seen.
    [1. Animals—Fiction.] I. Cushman, Doug, ill. II. Title.
PZ7.S346328 We 2003   [E]—dc21   2002004590

ISBN 978-0-8050-6167-3 / First Edition—2003 / Designed by Amy Manzo
Printed in September 2009 in the United States of America by Worzalla Publishing Company Ltd.,
Stevens Point, Wisconsin, on acid-free paper.

10 9 8 7 6 5 4 3 2

The artist used watercolor, pen and ink, and colored pencil
to create the illustrations for this book.

JOHN SCHINDEL
ILLUSTRATED BY DOUG CUSHMAN

What Did They See?

ANTIQUES
•
CURIOSITIES

Henry Holt and Company
New York

One day Raccoon found something
wonderful, something she had never
seen before.

She held it up.

She jiggled . . .

and wiggled,

and giggled,

and blinked her eyes.

"It's amazing!" said Raccoon.

She hurried to show Beaver.

Beaver looked at it this way, then that way, and smiled.

"That's a good-looking thingamajig," said Beaver. "Wow!"

They hurried to show Porcupine.

"Oh, look. Yes! Oh, my! It's a lovely whatchamacallit," said Porcupine.

"It's a good-looking thingamajig," said Beaver.

"I'm in love. It's amazing!" said Raccoon.

Raccoon, Beaver, and Porcupine
ran to show Otter.

Otter looked and looked, and sniffed
and looked, and was delighted! "It's a
dashing thingamabob!" said Otter.

"It's a lovely whatchamacallit, indeed!"
said Porcupine.

"I say it's a good-looking thingamajig!"
said Beaver.

"It's amazing!" swooned Raccoon.

They danced and they sang.
They shouted, "HOORAY!"

Then they had a parade, for it was the most amazing thingamajig whatchamacallit thingamabob any of them had ever seen.

And what each one saw was
something wonderful indeed.